The House at
Mingo Pond

LINDA HOFFMAN

PAGE PUBLISHING, INC.
New York, NY

First originally published by Page Publishing, Inc. 2015

ISBN 978-1-68139-876-1 (pbk)
ISBN 978-1-68139-877-8 (digital)

Printed in the United States of America

THAT HOUSE, THAT *EVIL* HOUSE. The dark, brooding, sinister house sat five hundred yards north of Mingo Pond. Stories had circulated for years that something terrible had happened on the dirt floor of the basement years ago. But no real evidence had ever surfaced. Now the kids just used the house as a test of courage. On Halloween, you had to run up onto the porch and stay there in the dark for one minute. Then, you had to throw a brick through the already broken windows and run away. It was all innocent fun. If the kids had only known what horrible things had happened there, they would have kept on running and never looked back.

The path to Mingo Pond had been overgrown with weeds, but that never stopped the kids from making their way down to the pond for a hot day's swim. They stayed as far away from the "spooky" house as they could. Even in the daylight, it sent a chill up their backs. When the daylight would fade, you could see the kids race out of the woods, not wanting to be anywhere near the house after sunset.

Christopher Wilson lived near the pond. The Wilson family had lived there for what seemed like forever. Christopher's parents had inherited the house on Willow Road after Grandma and Grandpa Wilson died in an automobile accident. Chris's dad had always loved Mingo Pond, so he brought Chris and his wife, Mary, to the family house. Mary, however, hated the Pond. She liked to have neighbors close by. You had to drive to the nearest house. Nighttime was the problem. It got so dark that it frightened her. Even the dog didn't like it there. Misty must have sensed the eerie vibrations that surrounded the Pond.

Christopher was six when they moved to the house. He thought it was cool. He would ride his bike and play with his friends, Jeffry "JJ" Johnston, Brian Manning, and Kenny Miles. Those guys were all the same age and got along great. Mary, Chris's mom, stayed home and took care of the house while his dad, Ed, worked in town at the corner garage.

Mary and Ed got married later than most couples. Ed was forty-two and Mary was thirty-six. Christopher was born almost nine months to the day after the wedding date. Ed was a hardworking husband and a basic provider. Mary had never dated much. Both of her parents were ill. She spent most of her life taking care of them. Her father died first of cancer; her mother the next year, Mary always thought, of a broken heart.

Mary met Ed when she took her car to the garage where he worked. He seemed like a gentle man with a great smile. She would find any reason to take a trip to town just to visit the garage. She'd bring him a home-baked pie or cupcakes, anything, just to see him. It wasn't love at first sight, more like two people hearing time ticking away and not wanting to be alone anymore. After Mary's parents passed away, they were married in a quiet civil ceremony. Not a storybook wedding, more like the joining of two people who would never be alone again. The birth of Christopher was a miracle to Ed and Mary. He had Ed's chin and Mary's smile and a head full of coal black hair. Mary had a rough delivery. The complications in the delivery room resulted in her having a hysterectomy. Thank God Christopher was all right. At least God gave her one beautiful baby. Mary vowed that nothing would ever happen to him as long as she lived.

After the accident that killed Ed's parents, the house sat empty. Ed just couldn't bear to sell it even though he knew Mary hated the idea of living by Mingo Pond. But work was slow at the garage and he was having trouble paying the mortgage on their small house. So after much pleading, Ed finally convinced her to move to his parents' house and give it a try. The money from the sale of their house was just enough to pay the balance of the mortgage with some extra money to pay late bills.

The house needed a lot of work. Ed did his best to make it sound and give it their personal touch, but he was careful not to make too many changes. He had grown up in that house and loved it the way it was. Although Mary hated the move, she did love the house. The veranda was the best feature. The porch wrapped around the house like loving arms, welcoming all who came to visit to sit and rest a while. And the living room, it was so large and cozy. Their furniture blended in nicely with the furnishings that had been left. If only the house was located somewhere else. If only the nights weren't so dark. If only the Pond wasn't so close.

Jeffrey "JJ" Johnston lived a short car ride away from the Wilson house. Steve Johnston bought the house as a fixer-upper to rent out but decided to live in it himself. Something about the Pond and the quiet appealed to him, and he wanted his family to experience "the simple life." Heather, JJ's mom, decorated the house with a warm country feel. A homebody by nature, she loved the idea of living away from the noise of the city. Besides, JJ would learn the benefits of country life. Outdoor play and fresh air, not stuck in the house. They could fish and swim and picnic by the Pond whenever they wanted. Before they moved in, they had heard the rumors about the house by the pond. Steve brushed them off as urban myth, but Heather wasn't so sure. It stood there so ominous and frightening. It almost seemed alive with evil. That house was the only part of the Pond she didn't like. As JJ got older, she warned him never to go near that house, ever.

Brian Manning lived in a trailer on a large plot of land closest to the pond. Joe, his dad, was in the process of building their house by hand. A carpenter by trade, he wanted his family to live in a house he built himself. Sara, his mother, worked right alongside her husband. Little by little, pay by pay, they worked on the house. Brian hated living in a trailer. All his friends had a house; he didn't understand how important it was for his dad to build their house by himself. Brian was quiet and self-conscious. He had a slight limp, a small birth defect. But he still rode his bike and played with the guys; he just couldn't run as fast as they could. It didn't bother the guys, but it bothered him.

He would sit by the pond and toss pebbles into it. The ripples spread out far and wide, keeping the reflection of the big house from being seen in the water. He didn't like that house. Too close to his, and way too creepy. His father had told him never to go near that house, and for sure, he never would. If anything would happen, he'd never be able to run fast enough to get away. Besides, that old house had secrets. He had heard the stories, and he wasn't going anywhere near it.

Kenny Miles lived almost directly behind JJ's house. It was a small house, almost a shack. Amy Miles was a single mother; no one knew who Kenny's father was. No one knew and no one asked. Amy wasn't the neighborly type. They said she had mental problems, but no one knew for sure. Kenny was very strange. He got along fine with the guys, but when his mother would call him to come home, his whole demeanor would change. He hated their house and his mother; she was so different than the other moms. And why didn't he have a dad? He was always afraid to ask his mom about him. One time when he did, she smacked his face and told him never to ask again.

Amy cleaned offices in town at night, that way she didn't have to talk to or see other people. Kenny had to tend the garden daily. Amy put up vegetables for the winter months. He also did the laundry and took care of the chickens. His mother would slaughter them after they were too old to lay eggs. Kenny hated the chickens. They were dirty and they smelled, and he hated to eat them, but he had no choice. Eat or starve, that was the rule. The only time he laughed was when he was with his friends, and for that small amount of time, he was a normal kid. But he always had to go home; he hated to go home, and he hated his mother.

NOW

THE SUMMER OF 1963 WAS a hot one. The thermometer soared into the nineties every day. Thank God for the pond. Swimming, fishing, and horsing around kept the guys occupied all summer. By now they were all, or near, fifteen. Chris's parents were the oldest of the group and the most stable. JJ's parents were the most fun. The guys could come over any time for a game of baseball in their big field. Brian's house was almost done. Soon he would live in a real house. Then, there was Kenny, so sullen and sad. Amy was sinking deeper into depression. Her actions were more violent toward him. He never told the guys, but they all knew. Everyone knew.

"Hey, JJ," Chris yelled. "Race you to the pond."

"You'll never beat me," JJ hollered as he rode his bike as fast as he could.

Brian was already at the pond waiting for everyone to show up. "What took you guys so long? I've been here an hour."

"I had to help my dad with the yard work," Chris explained. Then JJ explained similarly, "My mom needed me to clean up the basement. Where's Kenny? He should have been here by now."

"I haven't seen him today. I hope he's okay." Brian was worried about him. For the past couple of weeks, Kenny had been pretty quiet. JJ had noticed some bruises on his arms. Maybe he fell or maybe they were from his mom. None of them ever asked him how things were at home; they knew talking about his mother made him mad.

Kenny was trying to get out of the house, but Amy was having none of it. Chores needed done, and by the time they were done, it would be too late to meet the guys.

"Please let me go. I promise to get everything done when I get back. Please, let me go," Kenny begged.

"You think life is nothing but swimming and having fun…well, it isn't. You have to learn you have chores to do. You get these chores done or you'll not eat tonight," Amy yelled. Kenny flew through everything, got on his bike, and sped down the road before she could stop him.

"I don't care if I don't eat! I hate you!" he screamed at the top of his lungs.

Kenny arrived at the pond to see the gang waiting for him. *I don't know how I would survive my life without my friends*, he thought to himself.

"Hey, what took you so long? We almost came to get you," Brian yelled to Kenny.

"Please, don't ever come to my house. My mother would kill me if anyone came to get me. Please, promise you'll never come to my house," Kenny pleaded.

"Okay, Kenny. Calm down. We won't come over, all right? Are you okay?" Brian asked.

"Look," said Kenny, wanting to change the subject, "I came here for a swim. Last one in is a rotten egg!" They all jumped in the pond and swan till dusk. The way the sun was setting gave an eerie glow to the old house.

"We'd better get going home." Brian was afraid to be anywhere near that house at night. "It's getting dark, and my mom freaks out when I'm here after dark."

JJ laughed. "You guys aren't scared, are you?" Brian pressed further to leave as he got dressed. "Come on, guys. It's late, and you know we have to get back. Besides, I hate it here after dark."

JJ taunted, "You're all just a bunch of chickens! It's just a house."

"You've heard all the creepy stories about that house. It gives me the creeps," Brian said.

"Yeah, I've heard the stories, and that's all they are, creepy stories. You don't believe them, do you?"

"Yeah, I believe them," Kenny said seriously. "Something awful happened in that house years ago. I don't know what, but I know it was horrible."

"Maybe we should go in and investigate the house and see for ourselves," JJ said with a smirk, trying to convince them and himself.

"Forget it," Brian said. "I wouldn't go within ten feet of that place."

Kenny's expression was grim. "I'm telling you, guys, don't go near that place. It's evil!" With that statement, he hopped on his bike and sped off.

"What spooked him?" JJ said as he watched Kenny pedal down the path.

"I don't know, but I'm with him." Brian jumped on his bike then and was off. Whatever had freaked them out, Chris and JJ were not going to stay there alone.

THEN

HANK MILES WAS A MEAN man. His life as a child was hard. His father was abusive. The belt came down regularly for no apparent reason. The oldest of five sons, he got the brunt of the abuse. A man of foreign descent, his father ran the house with an iron fist, which was not limited to his children; his wife got beat on a regular basis as well. His father would drink every day. The more he would drink, the meaner and more abusive he got. Hank never cared one way or the other whether his father lived or died, and when he finally drank himself to death, it meant nothing to him. He felt even less concern for his mother. She never tried to stop his father from beating his children; he blamed her for not getting his father to stop the abuse. When Hank left home, he never looked back.

Esther Colby was a weak and cowardly woman. Jerome and Elizabeth Colby, her parents, were very religious, almost fanatical in their beliefs. Esther was plain—no makeup, hair pulled back into a tight bun, dark dresses, dark life. The family went to church every day plus prayed at home. Esther hated her life; she longed to be like the other girls. The only joy in her life was that she sung in the church choir. There, she felt free to let out all her pent-up emotions. Samuel Kirk was smitten with Esther. He too was raised in a strict home and hated it.

Esther walked to church for choir practice. Jerome had to tend the farm and allowed her that one bit of freedom. Samuel would meet her halfway, and they would talk. But one night, they didn't talk; they snuck into the old house by the pond and made love. Both guilt-ridden, they decided to never see each other again. Even though Esther was eighteen, she was dumb about womanly things. None of that was ever discussed in her house. Elizabeth told Esther when she got married she would know what to do.

Three months after the event at the house on the pond, she felt something was wrong, different. Too afraid to say anything to her mother, she hid her condition. Elizabeth noticed that Esther's dresses were fitting tighter. She was a thin girl, so any weight gain became quite obvious.

Jerome worked in the slaughterhouse in town. A very private man, he kept to himself, never making friends. There was one man, however, that Jerome did talk to and that was Hank Miles. A tall and brooding man, who did his job, never slacked off, and was always on time. Jerome admired that. Jerome mentioned his daughter Esther to him and, although he seemed interested, he never responded. He had nothing to give to anyone—no emotion, no tenderness, just nothing.

The conversation about Esther was brushed off until the day that Jerome discovered Esther's secret. Samuel had left town to join the army, never knowing of Esther's condition. He was killed in action. Esther was heartbroken, and by now, she couldn't hide her pregnancy anymore. Jerome was devastated. Never a violent man, he struck her for the first time.

"How could you do this? How could you be a whore?" Esther was sobbing as he continued, "You have sinned before God. You have disgraced our family. Who is the man who did this to you?"

She cried, "It was Samuel Kirk, and he died never knowing what my condition was!"

Jerome was pacing the floor, not sure what to do, but saying, "This is a blemish on my family. You have done this to me and your mother. Now, I will tell you what you're going to do." Jerome's thoughts turned to Hank Miles. A solid man, a hard worker; he would convince him, even pay him if he had to, to marry his daughter. That was the only way to hide the shame Esther had brought into the family.

Jerome rose earlier than usual the next day. He prayed to God to let Hank Miles be the answer to his problem as he went to work. The slaughterhouse reeked of blood and rotting meat. Hank was a man who didn't notice the smell at all. His life was as cold as the dead animals that hung in the lockers.

Jerome approached him as soon as he arrived. "Hank, I need to talk to you in private. Meet me outside at lunchtime." Hank was curious. What did Jerome need to say to him in private? When the whistle blew some time later, all the workers filed outside, away from the smell and the cold. Hank and Jerome met in the field behind the building.

"Hank, we need to talk. You seem like a just man and a hard worker and you appear lonely. I'm going to explain my needs to you, and if you agree, I will make sure you are well compensated."

Hank's curiosity was heightened by the word *compensated*. "What do you need from me, Jerome?"

"My daughter, Esther, has brought shame to my family. She is not married, but she is with child and the father is dead, never having known of her condition." Hank stepped back wondering what Jerome was going to ask him to do.

"I know you are single, and I know this may be a burden you may refuse to take on, but would you consider marrying my daughter? She is plain, quiet, and until now, never has done anything to disappoint our family. I will set you into a house by the pond, a small house, since I'm a man of small means. We will have you married in the next town. People will assume you two were married all along. I have no close friends, so no one will think much about the marriage."

Hank bristled at the thought of marrying an already soiled woman, but the thought of a house and someone to cook and clean for him was appealing. Hank paced the field in silence; Jerome hadn't asked him to love her, just take the shame off his shoulders. His mind started to race. Maybe he could marry that soiled whore and use her to do his bidding. She would have to do as he said; Jerome would never take her back home. His religion forbade divorce. She was just like his mother, a mealymouthed, plain, and weak woman. He'd use her all right, and she would have no choice.

If Jerome had known the kind of man he was giving Esther to, he would have killed her himself and saved her from the horrible fate that was to come.

They agreed to meet at Jerome's house on Saturday morning after church. Esther would not be going to church; she would stay home until she was married to Hank. Hank stood about six feet tall, had cold, lifeless eyes, and menacing presence. You could tell by looking at him that he had an evil streak. The way he looked through you, the way his eyes hid from your direct stare. He had secrets, but no one could have foretold how dark his secrets were.

Saturday morning Esther arose, sick to her stomach. She was having trouble sleeping and was not eating. The pregnancy was taking a toll on her, and she was so lonely. If only Samuel hadn't died, maybe her father would have let her marry him, and she would have been happy. She was terrified of the future. In fact, if she would have known the evil that was about to enter her life, she would have taken her own life and that of her unborn child. That would have been better than the horror that lay ahead of her.

Jerome and Elizabeth came home from church. Esther was seated in the parlor, having been told to be up and ready for company. They had not told her of their plan. That would be revealed when Hank arrived.

They all sat in silence until the knock on the door broke the quiet. "Jerome, shall I get the door?" Elizabeth asked.

"No. Stay seated. I will get the door." He opened the door and asked Hank in.

"Esther, this is Hank Miles. He is here at my request. He will be marrying you next week in the next county so no one will ask questions."

Esther's face turned pure white with fear. "Why, Father? I told you how sorry I was for shaming the family. Please don't make me marry a man I've never even talked to!"

"Be still! You have brought shame on our family. You will marry this man next week. You will be a dutiful wife, and you will never come back to live in this house again!" he spat. Esther turned and ran from the room, petrified with fear. One look at Hank was all it took to know her life was over.

"I'm sorry for her disrespectful display. We still have an agreement?" Jerome pleaded with Hank as he replied, "I will marry your daughter, and I will teach her the meaning of the word *respect*." After Hank left, Jerome and Elizabeth sat in silence. Esther cried—cried for her Samuel and for her uncertain future.

NOW

IT HAD BEEN AN UNUSUALLY hot summer at Mingo Pond. Fall would bring a welcome relief from the oppressive heat wave. The leaves were showing their colors early. Ed had always loved the fall season. The garage was hot and greasy, but the fall breezes meant an increase in work. Getting cars ready for the winter meant more money in the bank. It also meant late hours. Mary, however, hated the thought of fall and winter; it got darker earlier and that meant the eerie feeling of the Pond would also come back. The colors of the trees wouldn't mask the ominous feeling of the nights.

Having grown up in Mingo Pond, Ed had been aware of the stories surrounding the house by the pond, and as a boy, he had overheard his parents talking about the house. No one could say exactly what had happened there, but you just knew it had a presence of evil. The old house stood on the hill by the pond for as long as anyone could remember. The house was about one hundred years old, an estimated guess. The people that had lived there had long been gone, and for whatever reason, it was never occupied again. Ed, though not previously believing the stories, felt a little shaken lately whenever he even looked at the house. He tried to brush off the feeling, but for some reason, it hung over his head like a dark and threatening cloud.

Sitting on the veranda sipping hot apple cider in the crisp fall night air, Mary waited anxiously for Ed to come home from work. Chris was doing his homework and their new dog, Mandy, lay by his side. "Mandy, you don't like the night either, do you, girl?" Misty had died the year earlier, and Mandy was a sweet replacement. Ed's car pulled into the driveway, and Mary greeted him with a hug.

"Why are you out on the porch?" Ed asked inquisitively.

"I don't know," Mary replied. "Just wanted to take in the crisp night air, I guess."

"The night is beautiful…Look at the full moon," Ed continued.

Mary thought that was sweet. "Why, Ed Wilson, that almost sounded romantic."

"Can't a guy appreciate a beautiful night with his beautiful wife?" Ed smiled as he leaned over and tenderly touched her cheek.

"Sit down, and I'll bring you a glass of cider," Mary said as she got up and went toward the door.

"Make that hot cider. I feel a little chill," Ed asked as she went in the house. He gazed out toward the direction of the pond. What was bothering him today about that place? Why couldn't he shake that funny feeling? No wonder Mary hated that place; it was starting to give him the creeps too.

Mary came out and saw Ed gazing in the direction of the house. "What are you thinking about?" she asked.

"I don't know, Mary, maybe it's silly, but I've got a feeling about that house," he replied.

"See, I told you for years. I hated that place," Mary reiterated her fears.

Ed started to tell her what he saw the last time he took Chris to the pond to fish, "The last time Chris and I were at the pond, I could have sworn I saw someone come out of the house. Remember the night that Chris and I got back after dark? Just as we were leaving, I looked up, and I was sure I saw someone walking down the path behind the house."

Mary was feeling uneasy about Ed's seriousness. "Who do you think you saw?"

Ed thought. "I think it was a woman, but it was getting dark, and it caught me off guard to see a person there."

Mary asked, "Did Chris see anything?"

Ed looked somber. "I don't think so. I never mentioned the event to him. I think I'll mention something to Steve Johnston. He'll be in tomorrow to have his car serviced. And Joe Manning lives the closest to the pond, maybe he's seen something. You know, Mary, I've lived here all my life and never gave much thought to that place, but lately, I've gotten a feeling about it that I just can't shake. Come on. Let's go in. I'm getting cold. I don't want you to get a chill." Ed got up to go into the house.

"Too late, Ed Wilson," Mary replied. "That story you just told me sent ice-cold shivers down my back. You check things out if you want to, but keep Chris away from that place. If anything is happening there, I don't want my son put in harm's way. I told you a long time ago that place was evil. Now, I'm certain of it."

Joe Manning spent most nights working on finishing his house. Having not grown up by Mingo Pond, he had only heard the rumors about the house by the pond through casual conversations. Sara dismissed the stories as just that, stories. But lately, she had started to notice things that bothered her. Maybe it was just her imagination, but she could have sworn she had seen someone come and go late at night as she sat out on her porch.

"Joe, have you noticed someone at night, coming and going from the old house?" she asked.

Joe was now sure he had seen something as he replied, "I was just going to ask you the same thing."

Sara asked, "I wonder if someone bought the house and is fixing it up?"

"At ten o'clock at night? I doubt it. Besides, I've never seen a car or truck over there. How can you work on a place that big without tools and lumber? In all the years I've been working on our house, I've never seen anyone go there or maybe I just wasn't paying attention. Tomorrow I'm going to the garage to get some work done, maybe I'll mention something to Ed Wilson…or maybe I'm just paranoid," Joe replied.

Sara got up to go in the house. "Well, if you are, then it's catchy. Let's go in. Looking at that place just gives me the creeps." Joe looked past the pond and up to the house, shrugged his shoulders, and followed Sara inside. If only they had waited another minute, they would have seen a figure come out of the back of the house on the hill.

Heather Johnston had watched strange comings and goings from the Miles house ever since she moved in. Heather would see Amy return from work in town at about 9:00 p.m. every night. Then, she would leave out the back door, not to return until around midnight. Same thing every night. Odd, she thought, but then again, not so odd for a very strange woman. Lately, however, she had noticed her carrying shovels too. *I wonder what that crazy woman is doing,* she thought to herself. She never mentioned it to Steve; why bother him with such nonsense? Still, she was curious as to what was going on. Steve had noticed some activity as well.

"Hey, Heather," he called to her from the back porch, "what's that crazy woman up to every night?" It was ten o'clock and Amy was scurrying off, shovel in hand.

"I have no idea. I've seen her do that, night after night, for about a week," Amy told him.

Steve laughed. "Talk about a nut."

"I don't think it's funny," Heather said sternly. "Kenny lives in that house with a mentally unstable woman. No wonder that child looks so forlorn and lost. You can see the fear in his eyes. It makes me want to cry."

I wonder where she's off to every night, Steve thought.

"My worry," continued Heather, "is what she does to Kenny when she's at home. I've noticed some bruises on his arms and legs. I hope she's not abusing him."

Steve is now concerned. "Come to think of it, JJ's mentioned seeing some bruises too. But you know how boys are. Maybe he's just clumsy, always falling down."

Heather didn't agree with that. "Come on, Steve, he's fifteen years old, not two. A boy his age doesn't fall down that often."

Steve agreed, "I suppose you're right, but you don't really think she beats him, do you?"

She thought for a moment. "JJ said the other day that he had dark circles under his eyes and he's been losing weight." Her own words were starting to scare her.

"You know what, hon, I'm getting the car worked on tomorrow, and I'll ask Ed if he has any idea what is up with Kenny and his mom. Let's go in. The wind is turning crisp, and I'm tired," as he got up to go in and get a beer to calm his nerves.

"You have a beer and I'll have a glass of wine, and we'll both say a prayer that we're wrong." she answered, following him inside.

THEN

ESTHER CRIED HERSELF TO SLEEP. How could this be happening to her? She never meant to bring shame on her family. It was a mistake, and now she was going to have to marry this man with eyes of evil. How could her father do this to her? And her mother, she just sat silent, not stopping this horrible decision. If only someone could help. But there was no one. Just her and the baby she would bring into an uncertain life.

Hank had plans for this woman named Esther. He would not touch her until she had the bastard child, but after that, he would teach her the meaning of respect. *A stupid woman, just like my mother,* he thought.

The civil ceremony was somber to say the least. No religious ceremony for a soiled woman. God would never bless the union. Jerome kept his promise; he purchased a house for Hank. It was more like a shack, but it was a roof over their heads and that satisfied Jerome's debt to Hank. And Esther would never see them again. Elizabeth, in her heart, knew this was a bad mistake; but she could not go against her husband. That just wasn't done. As far as Jerome was concerned, he no longer had a daughter; she died the day she sinned.

The shack that Esther would be calling "home" was as cold and dead as her husband's eyes. A coal stove and an old ice box in the small kitchen and an outhouse next to the back door. Just a tub and small sink in the bathroom. Thank God there were two bedrooms. A single bed in one and a double bed in the other. *Please, God, let me sleep alone,* she prayed.

"You will sleep in the small room until you have that bastard child you're carrying. After that, you will come to me. Until then, talk as little as possible and expect nothing from me but your most basic needs," Hank stated coldly.

She closed the door to her room and sobbed uncontrollably. "What has my father done to me? How could he be so cruel?"

The winters by the pond were hard. The coal stove gave off meager heat, hardly heating one room. Between that and the pregnancy, Esther was ill most of the time. She did all the work around the house. Food was no problem. Hank liked to eat and made sure there was plenty of meat in the house. But Esther barely ate enough to keep herself alive. The stress of her condition took away her appetite.

"I didn't marry you to be sick all the time. If you don't start to eat, I will force food down your throat. You have chores to do, whether you're sick or not, so eat or I'll make you," Hank snarled at her one night after drinking his usual whiskey.

"I've been doing everything you've asked me to," sobbed Esther. "I'm going to have a baby and I'm ill."

Hank looked at her in disgust, "I told you before, that bastard child is not my concern, you can lose it for all I care. I'm not going to put up with your moaning and complaining. I will take the belt to you, pregnant or not!" He spit his foul breath in her face. Fear filled her soul.

He will beat me. I see it in his eyes, she thought to herself. "I won't complain anymore, I promise," she whispered.

"Well, see that you don't or you'll feel the snap of my belt," he growled. The rest of her pregnancy Esther kept as far away from Hank as she could. The evil in his eyes told her that he might kill her for nothing more than a complaint.

Roads were impassable, so Hank had to walk to the slaughterhouse every day. He rose at four a.m. and wouldn't return till dark. Then he would eat and drink himself to sleep night after night. Esther rose earlier than Hank. She would make the coffee and bake biscuits. She would go to the hen house and gather eggs for his breakfast. It was so hard to walk in the snow. She was now in her last month and the snow and the cold were killing her, but she couldn't complain. The fear she felt was real. Hank could care less about the child she was carrying. In fact, if he could, he would get rid of it and not think twice.

After Hank left, Esther went to the henhouse to clean the coup. "What is happening to me?" she said aloud. She reached between her legs and felt moisture. She stumbled back to the house through the snow, doubled over in pain. She had no way to call for help; no one was near to come to her aid. The pain was unbearable. No one had told her what to do. The baby was coming fast, and she was all alone. Esther lay on the cold floor and delivered her little girl. Cord and afterbirth still attached, she crawled to her bed and breathed life into her child. She carried the baby into the kitchen and cut the cord. She stumbled back to her bed and cradled her precious child to her breast; the one gift from Samuel that she had left. No one could take that from her.

Hank arrived late after trudging through the snow. "Esther," he growled, "where the hell are you, and where's my supper?" He opened the bedroom door and found her and the baby. "Finally, you've given birth to that bastard. What is it?"

Esther quietly answered, "A girl."

Hank laughed aloud. "Great, another stupid woman like you. You couldn't even have the right kind of baby. At least a boy would have earned his keep. Get up and cook my meal."

Esther pleaded, "I can't. I'm so weak." He leaned over and pulled her by her hair out of bed. She put the baby in the middle of the bed and slowly walked to the kitchen. *Oh, God,* she thought, *why are you punishing me? Why didn't you just let me die?* This would not be the last time she wished to die. It was only the beginning...

NOW

ED ARRIVED EARLY AT THE garage. Steve Johnston would be in to have his car serviced today, and he wanted to talk to him about the strange goings-on at the house by the pond. Steve too, was early, wanting to ask Ed the same thing. "Hi, Steve, you're early. Want a cup of coffee before we get started on the car?" greeted Ed.

"Sure, it's kind of chilly this morning. Fall will be brisk this year." Steve opened the conversation first. "Have you been down to the pond lately?"

Ed liked where this might lead. "Yeah, Chris and I went fishing there the other night. I don't mind the pond in the day, but at night, it gives me the creeps."

Steve continued, "Have you noticed anything unusual at the house on the hill?"

Ed was glad to hear this. "I'm glad you asked Steve. I told Mary I saw someone coming out of the house from around back. Seemed odd so late at night." Steve was relieved that he wasn't the only one, but his concern grew too.

"You know it's funny you mentioned that. Kenny's mother, you know the crazy lady, has been leaving her house every night for a couple of weeks and not coming back until about midnight. Heather saw her carrying shovels. I wonder what's up with that ...," Steve pondered.

"If you ask me," Ed said, "that woman should be committed."

Steve questioned Ed further, "Has Chris ever mentioned anything about the black-and-blue marks on Kenny's arms and legs?"

This was just getting more upsetting, thought Ed. "No, but I'll question him about it when I get home." Steve told him what

Heather noticed the last time Kenny came over to get JJ. "You don't think she beats him, do you?" Ed asked with concern.

"I sure as hell hope not, but if she is, we should do something about it." Steve was now wondering if Heather was right. "I think we should talk to Joe and Sara Manning. They live closest to the pond. Maybe they have seen something. Besides, I'd like to find out more about Amy Miles and her son." They agreed to meet at Steve's house on Saturday. Ed would call Joe and Sara and invite them over. Maybe they could all figure out what the hell was going on.

Chris, JJ, and Brian all met at the pond on Saturday morning. It was a crisp day, but the sun was warm, perfect fishing weather. None of the boys knew about the meeting to discuss Kenny, his mother, or the house. They just thought they were all getting together to congratulate Joe and Sara on finishing their house. Brian was always the first to arrive since he lived the closest. Chris was always next, then JJ, and Kenny would follow. But today, JJ arrived alone.

"Hey, JJ, where's Kenny?" Brian hollered from the edge of the pond.

"I don't know. I haven't seen him all week. He hasn't come to school." JJ and Kenny went to the same school; Brian and Chris went to a private school.

Brian was worried. "Is he sick? Maybe we should go to his house and check on him."

JJ knew that wouldn't be good. "You know how his mother is. She'd kill him if we went over there." JJ knew Kenny would get into big trouble if they checked on him. Chris rode up on his bike and asked about Kenny and was surprised at the answer.

"What do you mean he hasn't been to school all week? Let's go over, and see what's going on!" he urged.

JJ had to stop this. "Chris, we'll just get him in trouble. If Kenny doesn't show up at school on Monday, we'll go check on him, trouble or not." JJ made sense, even if they didn't like it, so they agreed to meet by the pond after school on Monday and then decide what to do.

THEN

JEROME AND ELIZABETH COLBY DIDN'T have a daughter anymore. After her sin, Jerome considered her dead. The pain and grief was too much for Elizabeth to take. She fell into ill health. They packed up and moved to her sisters so she could be taken care of. Never seeing their granddaughter, and never again seeing Esther.

With every passing day, Hank became more brutal. There wasn't a day that went by that he didn't hit or punch her. And the child… she too felt the wrath of his hands.

The years dragged on. One day to another, all the same…fear, terror, and abuse. Amy, the child, was slow. The hard birth did some damage, probably from lack of oxygen. The physical and mental abuse didn't help either. There would be no school for her; she would help do the chores and do Hank's bidding. As she grew, his bidding became more brutal and physical in nature. Esther was old before her time and was going mad. She rarely spoke, even to Amy. The many years of physical and mental abuse had finally taken its toll on her.

"You're just a waste of time," Hank would scream at Esther. "Look at you. I didn't think you could get any uglier than what you were. But I was wrong! You make me sick!" He would continue to scream at her, even after his whiskey was gone. He would force her to his bed and brutalize her. She would just lay there motionless, blocking out the pain. She didn't feel pain. Or maybe she was in so much pain, she was numb. He would make Amy watch. She just huddled in the corner and stared.

No one ever noticed that Amy didn't attend school. They just didn't want to get involved. She might have been slow, but she wasn't stupid. She was getting older and becoming fully aware of what was happening. Esther, at thirty-six, had been driven out of her mind. The years of abuse had made her shrivel up inside and out. Her pain would soon be over, and Amy's would then begin.

NOW

STEVE AND HEATHER PACED THE floor awaiting the arrival of their guests. "I hope that we can put the pieces of this puzzle together tonight," Heather said anxiously.

Ed and Mary were the first to arrive. "Hi, Ed, I'm so happy you and Mary could make it," Steve said as they shook hands.

"And, Mary, how are you?" Heather asked as they hugged.

"I've been better," Mary said. "This situation with Kenny has me unnerved."

"I'm worried about him myself. And if the marks on his arms and legs have anything to do with his mother, we'll have to stop it." Heather was almost shaking as she spoke. "Now, folks, let's wait till Joe and Sara get here, then, we can all compare notes."

Joe and Sara arrived just as Steve was pouring hot cider. "Boy, is it chilly! And the clouds are starting to gather." Ed was grateful for the warm drink. "Thanks for the cider." A knock on the door interrupted their conversation before it got started.

Joe and Sara entered and got some hot cider off the counter. Joe took a sip of cider. "I want to tell you, the weather sure has changed from this morning. It's really cold and the wind is starting to howl through the trees."

"Yeah," Sara said, "just another spooky fall night at the pond."

"Now, don't be so dramatic." Joe laughed.

"I'm serious," said Sara. "It gets so creepy down here in the dark."

Heather and Mary agreed. "Well, I want to say for the record that I've been getting a little freaked out myself lately." Ed was now serious. "Why don't we all go into the living room and get comfortable? I think we all have a lot to talk about." Steve motioned for everyone to go to the living room. He took a deep breath and wondered where this "conversation" was going to lead.

THEN

HANK MILES WAS BECOMING MORE deranged. The brutality he had been heaping on Esther was now much more cruel. He created his own private hell; no eyes prying into his business. Although Hank was becoming more brutal, Amy was becoming smarter. She knew that Hank would kill her if she ever spoke up to him. But how long could her mother hold out until she figured out what to do? With Esther near death, Hank's physical needs were being satisfied by Amy. She hated the son of a bitch but knew she had to keep him away from Esther who could never survive another beating.

"Get that stupid woman dressed," Hank scowled at Amy one night. "We have to go somewhere."

Amy dared to ask, "Where are we going?"

"Don't ask questions, just get her dressed," he said, showing more anger. The look in his eyes was that of a crazed animal.

Where is he taking us? she thought as she feared for their lives.

Hank had a sinister plan. Esther was barely alive. Why keep a woman who was of no use to him? Besides, Amy was taking care of his desires. But she had a spark of fire in her he had to kill. Unlike Esther, she was not weak and cowardly. Today, he had a plan to fix that for good. The plan he devised was so evil that only a person criminally insane would have concocted it. He needed to gain power over Amy; today he would gain that power and be rid of Esther forever.

NOW

IT WAS GETTING DARK. THE boys were tired and hungry. "Why don't we go to my house and get something to eat? I'm starved," Brian said as he packed up his fishing gear. "No one's home 'cause they all went over to your house. I guess to celebrate our finishing the house finally," he said to JJ.

"We'll have your whole house to ourselves. I hope you have plenty of food. I could eat a horse," Chris said. They all biked to Brian's house and started to raid the refrigerator.

"I wonder when our folks will get home," JJ said as he stuffed his face with potato salad.

"They're probably talking about how much work it was to build our house. I'm just glad I don't have to live in that trailer anymore." Brian laughed.

"Better to live in that trailer than in the shack that Kenny lives in," JJ said grimly.

"I really feel sorry for him. His mother's a nut!" Chris said loudly.

"Chris, you don't know the half of it. I've noticed her walking at night, going toward the house. I thought I had seen her when I was younger, but I never paid much attention. But lately, she's been carrying shovels and staying there until about midnight." JJ was looking at the house with a pained look on his face.

"Why didn't you say something before?" Chris asked.

JJ answered, "Hey, she's crazy. We all know that. I just thought it was some nutty thing she does."

Brian looked over to JJ and said, "I think I saw her too!"

Chris looked stunned at the news: "Am I the only one who's never seen this?"

"I'm not sure what I saw," Brian continued, "but lately, I've seen someone coming and going late at night into that house. I can see it from my bedroom window. I can't say who I've seen, but someone's been in that house." They all stood silent. What had Kenny's mother been up to? Where had Kenny been? Maybe it was time to search *that house* by the pond for some answers.

THEN

AMY DRESSED ESTHER, BUT IT wasn't easy. Hank had beaten her several days earlier and broke her ribs. She had been coughing up blood and was in a lot of pain. Amy had tried to stop Hank and was knocked unconscious. When she woke up, she found him passed out and Esther moaning in pain.

The snow was deep, and the wind was blowing large drifts. "Why don't you tell me where we're going?" Amy pleaded.

"You'll see soon enough. Now shut up and keep walking!" His eyes were glazed over with evil.

As they came to the pond, ice formed in Amy's veins. What was he going to do with them? Why were they at the pond? She tried to run, holding her mother under her arms, but they fell into a snow bank.

"You can't run away from your fate," Hank screamed. "Your destiny is mine!" He grabbed Esther. Amy tried with all her strength to stop him, but his might was stronger than hers and Amy crumbled into the snow. She could see a hole had been chopped in the ice. Hank dragged Esther by her hair.

"You were nothing but a soiled woman when I married you. I have no use for you any longer. Now meet your fate!" He howled to the sky as he held Esther's head under the water. Ice forming on his face, he looked like the devil incarnate. Esther's limp body lay on the ice. Amy ran to help her mother, but Hank knocked her down. "If you don't do as I say, I will kill you right here. Make no mistake. Your life is now mine!" Holding Amy by her hair, half dragging her, half pushing her, he made her drag Esther's body to the old house on the hill. He had been there earlier and lit the way to the basement.

A grave had already been dug in the basement floor. He made Amy place her mother's lifeless body in the hole.

"Remember this day. Your fate has been sealed. You will join that useless woman in that hole if you don't do as I say. No one will know and no one will care, either. You're mine now, and I will kill you like I did her!" He stood there and laughed as he made Amy bury her mother. It would not be the last time they would come to that house. The *evil* had just begun.

NOW

"I THINK WE ALL KNOW why this meeting is taking place," Steve said seriously. "Heather and I are concerned about Kenny Miles and his mother. Heather has noticed bruises on his arms and legs and, as I understand, some of you have too. Some of us have also noticed strange activity at the abandoned house by the pond. What are your suggestions on how to handle this situation?"

Ed spoke up first, "I saw someone come out of the house one evening when Chris and I were night fishing. I thought it was a woman, but I can't be sure."

Joe jumped in, "Sara and I live closest to Kenny's house, and we've both seen Amy Miles leave her house after nine at night and not return until after midnight. I have no idea how long this has been going on. Maybe I should have been more observant. The past several nights she has been carrying shovels. What do you think she's up to?"

Mary spoke next, "Why don't we go to the old house and see if anything is wrong?"

"Why don't we confront Amy and ask her what the hell is going on?" was Heather's suggestion.

"Steve," Ed asked, "have you seen Kenny lately?"

"Come to think of it, no," Steve answered. "In fact, JJ said he hasn't been to school for about a week. Maybe he's ill."

"Or maybe something terrible has happened to him," Mary started to cry.

"Okay, honey, we're all here to try and figure things out, just calm down." Ed tried to calm Mary down. The "things" that were happening were way beyond anything they could have imagined. Soon all the evil would be revealed.

THEN

Amy was both numb with cold and terror. There was nowhere to run. The heinous crimes that had been heaped on her mother were now coming her way.

Hank wasn't stupid. He knew that if she had the chance, she would run away or kill him. He already planned what he was going to do. The slaughterhouse had heavy chains and locks. He had taken a chain and a lock; he knew to what use he would put them.

There was a coal cellar in the shack. As Amy was dragged into the house that evening, her fate became known.

"You think for one minute I'm going to leave you alone so you can run away? I told you that you're mine, and you will live as I say."

One night, as she slept, he must have put the chains in the coal cellar. The chains were secured to the beams. There would be no escape. In the night, she would be chained to his bed, so he could do as he pleased with her. In the day, while he worked, she would stay in the coal cellar. She dared not fight or the same fate her mother met would be hers. From that day on, Amy thought of nothing else but how to kill Hank Miles.

"No one knows and no one cares," he had said. His own words would someday come back to haunt him.

NOW

STEVE, ED, AND JOE SET their plan into motion. They would first talk to their sons and try to find out what they knew about Kenny's relationship with his mother. Next, the men would go to the house and watch for whoever was going there at night. Third, Steve and Heather would call the rest of them the minute they saw Amy leave her house at night. Satisfied that they had made progress, Ed and Mary left. Joe and Steve set up a signal call to alert each other that Amy was on the move.

Joe talked to Steve, "We're really concerned how this might affect the boys. They're so close to Kenny. If anything happens, I don't want them involved."

"Don't worry," Steve replied, "Heather and Sara and Mary won't let anything happen to the boys. I wouldn't want to be the person who tries to hurt Brian, Chris, and JJ with those three women protecting them."

With the plan set, everyone returned to their homes to start the mission. "I hope this works. I would like to get back to a normal life," Heather said as they shut the door.

"Hon, I don't know where this is going, but I'll tell you one thing, none of us are going to let that boy get hurt. We'll help him, or we'll die trying."

THEN

AMY'S LIFE DETERIORATED INTO A never-ending stream of torture. Hank was drunk with power. The abuse was more violent and never ending. Something was happening to Amy. She was ill; every morning was nonstop nausea. *Oh my god,* she thought, *I'm pregnant. That son of a bitch made me pregnant!* The fear was consuming her. It was now time to make a plan. How could she kill Hank?

The only chance she had would be at night. He would assault her then drink whiskey until he passed out. If only she could figure out a way to get him to unlock her chains. Her opportunity came one night when she least expected it. Hank came home from the slaughterhouse early. He opened the coal cellar door and dragged her up the steps.

"Fix my supper. I'm tired of cooking my own food. If you do anything, I'll break your legs and you'll never walk again." He had already been drinking and was staggering around the kitchen. He chained her legs to the pipes under the sink and watched her every move. But he was too drunk to stay awake. He passed out in the chair.

Think, Amy, think! Here's your chance. Her chains didn't reach to the living room. But maybe she could get the pipe off. Hell, she'd bust them if she had to. After about an hour, she was able to pry the pipe loose. For the first time in a year, she was free of her chains. *I'll fix him for what he did to my mother. I won't kill him, but I'll make him wish he was dead.*

She took a pot off the stove and bashed Hank in the head until she fell to the floor exhausted. Blood was spattered over the floor, the ceiling, and herself. But he was still alive. She wasn't done with him yet, not by a long shot. It became clear to her exactly what she would do with Hank Miles. He would suffer the way he had made her mother suffer. She wouldn't let him die; she'd just make him wish for death.

Amy put on her boots and waited for nightfall. She packed a bag with the chains, the bucket from the coal cellar, and an oil lamp. She made a litter out of some lumber and blankets. She tied his unconscious body to the litter and set out for the abandoned house. The cold night air revived her soul.

"I'll teach you the meaning of respect," she said as she dragged the litter slowly to the house on the hill by the pond.

Her new-found energy made her load lighter. She was careful no one saw her. She reached the house and took the litter inside. She lit the lamp and opened the door to the basement. She took the litter and slid it down the steps. She wasn't taking any chances of Hank waking up, so she hit him again with a piece of wood she found in the wood box.

"You son of a bitch, you won't wake up until I want you to." She laughed as he lay bleeding.

She rolled him off the litter and found the support beam. Not only would she chain him, she would break his fingers to make sure he couldn't undo the chains. She looked at the evil man named Hank Miles, the man who had brutalized her mother and raped her repeatedly.

"You may have killed my mother, but as God is my witness, what you did to her is nothing compared to what I have planned for you!" Amy made sure Hank was still breathing and left. "You better live because I have plans for you." She laughed. "Now, Hank, don't disappoint me!"

She returned to the shack she called home. If only she wasn't pregnant. If only she would have been able to run away. But now, she had a new mind-set. Make Hank pay for all the abuse he had heaped on her and the murder of her mother. And for sure, he definitely would pay.

NOW

MONDAY MORNING CAME WITH NO Kenny at school. JJ couldn't wait for school to let out so he could see the guys. "Where is he? Why isn't he in school?" Steve was waiting for JJ to come home from school. He wanted to find out about Kenny. JJ opened the door to find Steve in the kitchen.

"Hi, Dad, can I go fishing with the guys?"

"Sure, son," Steve replied then added, "Is Kenny meeting you guys?" He didn't want to come right out and ask about Kenny, not yet.

"I don't know, Dad. I haven't seen him for a week. He hasn't been in school." This was not the answer that Steve had hoped for.

"He hasn't been in school for a whole week? Did any of you go to his house to see what's wrong?" he asked. Steve didn't like the sound of this.

"No, Dad, we can't. His mom would be real mad if we came over. We've never been allowed."

Steve hadn't heard about this. "What do you mean?"

JJ tried to explain what he knew, "All he said is that his mom would kill him if we ever came to his place."

Steve didn't want to get into it any further for now. "Okay, go fishing. And if you see Kenny, just let me know."

"Dad, why are you asking about Kenny? Are you worried about him?" JJ asked.

Steve had to tell him something. "Let's just say, I'm concerned."

"Okay, Dad, I'll tell you if I see him," JJ said as he grabbed his fishing gear and sped off to the pond.

Brian ran into his house and asked if he could meet the guys at the pond. Joe asked Brian if he had seen Kenny too. He told his dad that he was a little worried because he hadn't seen him for a week.

"Why don't you check with JJ and see if Kenny has been at school today?" asked Joe. Brian told his dad that on Saturday JJ said that Kenny hadn't been to school in a week either. "Are you worried about Kenny, Dad?"

Joe replied, "I'm a little worried. Your mother and I noticed the bruises on his arms and legs. We just wanted to make sure that he's okay." Joe didn't want to upset Brian, but it was obvious that something was terribly wrong. Brian left hoping JJ would tell him he had seen Kenny.

Ed and Mary were at the kitchen table when Chris got home from school. "Chris, can Mom and I talk to you a minute?"

"Sure, Dad, what's up?" Chris was not sure what was going on.

"Brian and JJ's parents and us…we are all pretty worried about Kenny. Have you seen him lately?"

Chris answered, "No, Dad, he hasn't been to the pond for a week, and JJ said he hasn't been to school either. Do you think something's happened to him?"

Ed asked more, "Have any of you guys seen anything strange at the abandoned house by the pond?"

Chris had a scared look on his face. "Brian mentioned something Saturday. He said he'd seen someone going to the house late at night. He can see the house from his bedroom window. He couldn't make out who it was, but he's sure someone's been coming and going regularly. JJ said he's seen Kenny's mother leaving at night, about nine o'clock for as long as he can remember. What do you think is going on?"

"I'm sure there's a logical explanation," Ed said but wasn't so sure himself, "but see if JJ has seen Kenny." Chris got his stuff and biked as fast as he could to meet the guys.

"I'm calling Steve and Joe," Ed said to Mary. "We've got a big problem on our hands."

THEN

AMY WALKED TWO MILES INTO town to look for work. It was the first time in her life that she was away from the pond. A man from the slaughterhouse had come to the shack looking for Hank. He had never missed work, not one day, and they wondered what had happened. Amy explained that he left to take care of his sick mother. Amy laughed. *He won't be coming back.*

She needed money, and with no education, the only work she could find was cleaning. She went from place to place until finally she got a job. She worked at night, five to nine, seven days a week. It didn't pay much, but she didn't need much. The shack had the coal stove, and she had the chickens and the garden.

For as slow as she was, she learned fast. She still had to keep Hank alive. Her obsession with his torture kept her alive. Besides, the baby was due in spring. No one would ever find out she was pregnant. She'd make sure of that.

Her nightly trek through the woods to the house by the pond brought out as much evil in her as she ever saw in Hank.

"You bitch," Hank would scream at her. "Why don't you just kill me? You know you want to kill me."

She screamed back, "That's where you're wrong, Hank Miles. I don't want you dead. I want you alive to suffer more than you ever made me or my mother suffer. Now you'll feel the snap of my belt!"

She would beat him until her arms would go numb. He would scream in pain. Not enough to kill him, just enough to make him lapse in and out of consciousness. She would bring him rotten food to eat and just enough water to keep him alive. He would sit for days in his own filth. Yeah, he wished for death, but that wouldn't come for many years.

Amy delivered her baby in the spring the same way her mother had delivered her, alone. If only it would have been a little girl. But it was a boy, Hank Miles's son. She would never love this child from rape. Not *his* child. But she would raise him, and when she felt the time was right, he would join Hank Miles. After all, like father, like son.

NOW

THE GUYS MET AT THE pond, each one more concerned than the other. "Have you seen Kenny?" Brian yelled to JJ as he arrived on his bike.

"No," JJ yelled back to Brian. "He still wasn't in school today."

Chris arrived in the middle of their conversation. "My parents are pretty worried about Kenny," he told them.

"Yeah, mine too," said JJ and Brian in unison.

"Look, we said we'd go check on him if he didn't show up at school today, so let's go," Chris said.

JJ was ready to go over to Kenny's house and find out. "What if his mother is home? She'd never let us in to see him."

Brian was shaking at the thought of a confrontation with Amy Miles. "Look," Chris said, "the only way we're going to know if Kenny's all right is to go to his house and check."

"All right, then…Let's go," they all replied hesitantly.

THEN...
TO NOW

AMY DID ENOUGH TO KEEP Kenny alive. She breast-fed him but never bonded with him. Her heart had died years ago. She had turned into another Hank Miles: cold, heartless, and as dead as the carcasses at the slaughterhouse. She would keep Kenny alive; she would keep Hank alive. Her hatred for both of them fed the evil that was in her heart.

Her nightly raids at the house sent her into a rage. All her frustrations and anger were heaped on Hank. She broke his leg one night with a pipe, and another night, she shattered his foot. "You think you can get away, but you never will. You're mine, and I'll do with you as I wish!" Screaming at him as he had done to her, she would laugh at his pain, relish in his agony. Days turned into years.

In spite of the abuse, Kenny grew into a young man. He never told anyone of the things his mother did to him. The beatings and the mental abuse were dished out on a daily basis. He kept all of that to himself. Mingo Pond was more populated than before; Amy had to send Kenny to school. Prying eyes were not what she wanted. She had a mission, and nosy neighbors didn't fit into her plan.

After fifteen years, she was growing tired of Hank Miles. Maybe it was time for her to fulfill her evil end. And Kenny, he had a fire that needed to be put out. Hank had thought that of her not too long ago as well. *Smart-mouthed little bastard,* she thought to herself, *just like that son of a bitch that's his father. I have no use for either one of them anymore.*

She had lured Kenny to the house late one evening a week ago. She told him that she had planted a garden there. and it was time to harvest it. He was terrified, as always, to tell her no. Her beatings had been more frequent, and she hardly gave him anything to eat. Maybe if he just went with her, she would leave him alone. He had to get up the courage to go near the house, especially at night. He would soon know why he had a reason to be scared to death.

NOW

THE BOYS BIKED TO KENNY'S house just before dusk. They were so afraid of what they would find that none of them wanted to knock on the door. "Kenny, are you in there?" JJ yelled through the open window. No answer.

"Come on, Kenny, open the door," Brian hollered. Chris decided to break the window. "We're going to get in big trouble for this," Brian said.

"I don't care. If Kenny's in trouble, we have to help him," answered Chris. They all went in to find no one there, but they did find blood on the kitchen floor.

"That's it! I'm going to get my dad!" JJ said as he ran out and jumped on his bike to his house.

"What happened here?" Chris said.

"I don't know, but I think we'd better leave this up to our parents now," Brian said as they decided to wait for JJ to come back with his dad.

"Dad, Dad! Come quick! We broke into Kenny's house and there's no one there, but there's blood on the kitchen floor!" JJ yelled as he ran into the house.

"What do you mean, you guys broke in?" Steve hopped up from the chair.

"Come on, Dad. This is bad, real bad!" JJ's begged his dad to come quickly.

"I'm calling Ed and Joe to meet us there. Just don't go anywhere without me." Steve called the men and told them to meet him at Kenny's house. He and JJ got in the truck and sped down the road.

As Kenny and Amy arrived at the house by the pond, Kenny was trembling. *Why would she plant a garden here?* he thought.

"Let's take a look inside," Amy told Kenny.

He was very reluctant. "I don't want to go in that house. I never want to go in that house."

"I said, let's go in the house." Her eyes glared at him with hatred. Before he had a chance to run, Amy hit him with a piece of wood on the back of the head. She dragged him down the steps to the basement and chained him next to the father he had never met.

"Well, don't you two make a pair?" She laughed out loud. Hank, by now, was skin and bones. He was deranged and near death. She grabbed his filthy hair and looked him in the blank eyes and said,

"I told you you'll die when I say you'll die and not one minute sooner. Open your eyes and say hello to your bastard son!" she screamed in his face. She smacked Kenny's face to wake him into consciousness. "Come on, Kenny, say hello to your daddy."

As the fog lifted, he looked in horror at the man chained next to him. The stench was overpowering, and he gagged.

"What are we doing here? Why have you chained me next to this man?" Kenny was sobbing in terror.

"Well, you've always wanted to meet your father, so I brought you to him. This is your dear old dad. I'm going to make you do to him what he made me do to my mother." She pointed to the spot where Esther had been buried. Amy pulled out a butcher knife and grabbed Hank by his hair.

"Wake up, Hank! It's time to meet your fate. You're useless to me now!" She lifted his head and slit his throat. Her eyes were glazed over with evil.

Kenny turned away and threw up. "My god, you killed him. How could you kill him?"

"You'll bury him just like he made me bury my mother. Then you will stay here until I decide to kill you." She had chained his feet tightly together so he couldn't run. The hole had been dug days earlier, all he had to do was lift him up and throw him in the hole and cover him with dirt...just as she had done with her mother's body, fifteen years earlier.

Someone will come to find me, he thought to himself. *They have to…or she'll kill me just like she killed the man she said was my father.* Frozen with fear, he did what he was told. The look in his mother's eyes told him she would kill him right there if he even said one more word. *God, please help me. I'm so frightened. I don't want to die,* he prayed as she chained him tighter to the beam.

Ed, Mary, Steve, Heather, Joe, and Sara all met at Kenny's house. The boys were extremely anxious waiting for their parents to arrive. Brian ran to his dad and stumbled into his arms. "Dad, something awful has happened I just know it. There's blood all over the floor."

"Now let's not jump to conclusions," Ed said. "Maybe she slaughtered a chicken for dinner and got blood on the floor."

"Maybe she did, but then, where's Kenny, Dad?" Brian pleaded.

"Okay," said Steve. "Let's all go to the house by the pond. If she's been going there at night, maybe we'll find her there and find out what's been going on."

Heather spoke up, "I don't want the boys to go anywhere near that place," Mary and Sara agreed.

"If Kenny's in trouble, we want to be there to help. We're old enough. Besides, he's our best friend. Please, Dad, don't make us stay away," Chris pleaded with his dad.

"All right," Joe said, "but you boys stay out of our way."

"We will, Dad," Brian said.

The moon was casting an ominous glow on the house. Ed, Joe, and Steve took a deep breath and climbed the hill to the house. The boys stayed a safe distance behind, but they were ready to help if they were needed. None of them were prepared for what they were about to find.

Ed, Steve, and Joe walked carefully up the rotten steps to the porch. "Be quiet," Ed motioned. "If anyone is in there, we don't want them to know we are here."

Steve apprehensively walked over to the door. "Hey, guys, there's some kind of light coming from the back of the long hallway." Joe and Steve moved closer to see. "Well, someone is definitely in there." Ed was very nervous. *Who could it be?*

The boys were getting anxious too. "What's taking so long?" JJ asked with a quiver in his speech.

"They can't just barge in. What if someone has a gun or a knife or something?" Chris whispered.

Brian was worried about his dad. "Maybe we should have called the police."

"There was no time. What if Kenny's in danger? They had to find out right away. Don't worry Brian, our dads won't let anything happen," JJ assured him.

Amy had deteriorated into the same crazed animal that Hank had been all those years before. Looking at Kenny was like looking at Hank Miles. The hatred for him was the same hatred she had for Hank.

"You are the bastard son I had because of that son of a bitch," she screamed, pointing toward Hank's hand-dug grave.

"I had you because he raped me. I never wanted you. I don't want you. After I kill you, I'll be free for the first time in my life. But before you die, I'll make you suffer like I've suffered. Your fate is in my hands, and you'll pray for death!" The evil spouting out of Amy made Kenny know his life would soon be over.

Joe, Ed, and Steve formed a plan. They would quietly pry the door open and slowly go toward the dim light and muffled voice. The hinges were rotten, so they carefully removed the door. Amy was so out of her mind that she never heard the noise on the porch.

But Kenny had heard it. *God, please let someone come. Please let them know I'm here*, he prayed silently. Amy was pacing the dirt floor, fondling the knife she had used to kill Hank. "Your blood will mix with your fathers and justice will finally be done!"

JJ couldn't wait anymore. "I'm going to see what's happening. If Kenny's in there, I have to help him."

Chris agreed but Brian was terrified. "I can't run. You know my leg is bad. I'll never be able to run away if there's trouble."

"Look, Brian, stay behind me," Chris said. "If anything happens, JJ and I will handle it, and you run to your house and tell our moms to call the police."

Slowly the boys climbed the steps to the porch. They saw that their dads had removed the door. "I can't see our dads," JJ said, "but I see a light at the end of the hall."

"Let's go slowly and see where they went." Chris was frightened, but if Kenny was there, they were determined to help.

The men reached the top of the steps to the basement. "Someone is down there," Ed whispered.

"You're right about that, now what?" Steve whispered back.

"The steps look rotten. I don't know if they'll hold all our weight," Joe worried.

"I'm lighter than both of you," Steve said. "I'll go first and test the steps."

"You think anyone will care if you're missing? No one knows, and no one cares!" Amy was using the same words that Hank Miles had said to her.

Steve crept down the steps, careful not to make any noise. "Come on." He waved to the men. As he reached the bottom of the steps, he saw Amy pacing the floor, wildly swinging a butcher knife in the air. The light from the candles showed her face.

"That woman is going to kill Kenny," Steve said to Ed who was right behind him. "You startle her, and Joe and I will jump her."

Just as they reached the bottom of the steps, Amy saw them. She ran full force at Steve. Her eyes were glazed over with evil. The boys heard the commotion and ran down the steps, but Brian tripped. They all tumbled down, knocking Ed and Joe to the ground. Steve tackled Amy, her arms swinging wildly, slashing him in the face.

She howled like a crazed animal as she swung the knife some more. Ed and Joe regained their composure and ran to help Steve.

"Grab her arms, Joe," Ed yelled. As they fought with all their might, JJ, Chris, and Brian went over to try and free Kenny. "She killed my father," he screamed, "and she was going to kill me too!"

"Don't worry, Kenny, we'll get you loose." JJ found a key near the coal stove in the corner.

"Come on. Let's get him out of here!" Chris grabbed Kenny and put him over his shoulder and ran toward the steps.

50

Amy was rabid with fury. Her lips were covered with foam. She had finally gone totally mad. "You'll not take me alive!" she screamed. "I have to kill that bastard child to end the evil his father started!"

She had kicked Ed and broken some ribs, and she stabbed Joe in the arm. Steve's face was bleeding. He could hardly see through the blood in his eyes, but they ran to save their children.

"Chris, run faster. She's right behind us!" JJ was trying to help Chris carry Kenny. Brian stumbled and fell. Chris put Kenny down and ran back to get Brian back on his feet. JJ ran to help too. Amy reached the top of the steps just as Brian fell.

She lunged at him but missed. She was wild with insanity. "I'll kill you all. The evil stops here!" She screamed as she swung the knife. The men reached the top of the steps as Amy was screaming at the top of her lungs.

"Chris, get out of here. All of you get out of here," Ed yelled at the top of his lungs. Chris grabbed Kenny, and they all ran for their lives. JJ helped Brian run out the door.

The men were trying to subdue Amy. She swung the butcher knife blindly. "I'll kill you all. You're all evil. Justice is mine! Meet your fate!" Just as she swung the knife at Ed, Steve and Joe tackled her feet. She spun around and fell to the ground, the butcher knife piercing her chest.

Blood gushed from her mouth. She looked Ed right in the eyes and whispered, "I told you the evil stops here," and with that statement, she took her last tortured breath.

JJ, Brian, Chris, and Kenny ran back to Brian's house. "Mom, call the police. Dad needs help. Hurry!" Brian was crying so hard, Sara barely understood him.

"Hurry, Mrs. Manning, my dad and Joe need help!" Sara called the police and told them to come quickly. "Go to the abandoned house at Mingo Pond. Something terrible has happened. Please hurry."

Mary stayed with the boys as Heather and Sara ran to the house. "Oh my god, Joe, you're bleeding! What happened?" Sara asked as she reached the house.

"Don't go in there. Amy Miles is dead," Ed said as he helped Steve wipe the blood out of his eyes. Ed was doubled over in pain. Heather helped him to sit down.

"Sara," Ed called, "if we wouldn't have gotten there, Amy would have killed Kenny. She went completely insane. She evidently killed a man in the basement and was going to kill Kenny as well."

"I think the man was Kenny's father. She kept saying that she had to stop the evil that he had started," Joe said in a shaky voice.

The investigation the police did revealed the bodies of Esther and Hank Miles. The coroner's report stated that Esther had drowned and been abused for years. It also showed that Hank Miles had been tortured for years and the cause of death was a slit throat. Amy's death was ruled accidental. She fell on the knife that she had used to kill Hank Miles.

What now would become of Kenny? Who would take care of this poor abused child? Steve and Heather had wanted more children, but it just never happened.

"Heather, do you think we have room in our hearts for another child?" Steve was hoping Heather would say yes.

"Oh, I think we have lots of room. Are you asking if we can adopt Kenny?" she asked.

Steve was delighted at her reaction. "It will be a big responsibility, but JJ is his best friend, and I think we can make it work."

"Well, Steve Johnston," said Heather, "if you think it can work, then let's do it."

Kenny was placed in the hospital to be examined. Years of abuse showed up on the x-rays. The boys saw him every day. "I knew you guys wouldn't let anything happen to me," Kenny told them when they had come to visit.

"Hey, we have a lot more swimming and fishing to do, and we can't do it without you. Besides," JJ said, "I have to take care of my new brother, don't I?"

Kenny was confused. "What do you mean 'new brother'?"

"Well," said JJ, giving him the good news, "my mom and dad want you to come and live with us. They're going to adopt you."

Kenny couldn't contain himself any longer. Crying, he said, "You mean I'm going to have a real house and a mom and dad?"

"And don't forget a new brother," said JJ.

"Hey, what about us?" Brian said, "We're a part of this too."

"Yeah," said Chris, "we're the four musketeers. One for all and all for one!" They put one hand on top of the others and swore that no one and nothing would ever separate them again.

EPILOGUE

WHEN THE POLICE DUG UP the bodies of Esther and Hank, two other skeletal remains were found. According to historical records from the 1840s, Caleb and Emma Mingo, the founders of Mingo Pond, had disappeared under mysterious circumstances. The police determined that the remains were those of Caleb and Emma Mingo. The abandoned house always had an air of mystery about it, but the house at Mingo Pond had kept its secret until that fateful night.

The kids don't go there anymore. The mystery is now fact. Boarded up, it stands with all of its evil at the top of the hill overlooking the pond. No more windows to break, no more tests of courage. No one dares go there anymore.

HISTORY

CALEB AND EMMA MINGO FOUNDED Mingo pond in the early 1820s. Caleb was a powerful coal mine owner. He was ruthless in his running of the mines. He cared less about safety and more about profit. Emma was a meek and mousy woman. Caleb married her as a matter of convenience. He needed someone to cook and clean and bear him a son to carry on the family name. Love didn't figure in his life. Success and power were the only two emotions he could relate to.

Emma bore him one son then stopped having relations with Caleb. She fulfilled her duty to provide him with an heir; she would no longer share a bed with a heartless, cold man. Caleb raised Edward in his image. Self-centered and spoiled as a child; mean, cruel, and greedy as a young man. Both Edward and Caleb had no use for Emma. She was there to now serve both of them, more like a slave than a wife and mother.

Edward was educated in the finest school money could buy. He was clothed in custom-made suits and rode pure-bred horses. He showed little interest in running the mines and more interest in women and gambling. His father was determined to have him be the heir to the mine, but Edward wanted to leave Mingo Pond and spread his wings out West. Emma and Caleb had to leave Mingo Pond to visit Emma's family in Jackson County. Her mother was seriously ill, and Caleb saw the opportunity to meet new coal customers. Caleb put Edward in charge of production at the mine. Edward knew what to do. He knew how dangerous the mines could be, but he didn't care. He saw Caleb leaving as a time to party without prying eyes.

Edward bid Emma and Caleb good-bye at the train station and left to go to Walkerville to meet friends for a week of drinking, gambling, and women. While he was in Walkerville, a horrible accident took place at the mine. A methane gas explosion destroyed the mine and killed all the miners. How could this happen? How could life be so perfect one minute and so destroyed the next?

Edward arrived to turmoil. Emma and Caleb were notified and started their journey back to Mingo Pond. Because he wasn't there to take care of the mine, the blame was heaped on to Edward's shoulders. Families were up in arms, wanting restitution for the loss of their loved ones. Customers wanted their coal, and creditors want to be paid. Caleb wasn't one for banks. He trusted no one but himself with his money. He paid all of his bills in person and with cash.

Hidden deep in the basement at the house at Mingo Pond was a coal cellar with a small vault in the wall. Caleb and Edward were the only people who knew of the vault. That vault was Edward's way out. He blamed his father for making him be responsible for the mine. He blamed him for making him stay at Mingo Pond. He wasn't going to lose the life he wanted; he would take what was his and leave no one behind to accuse him of not doing his duty. He took all the money and his possessions and hid them in the woods. Holding a double-barreled shotgun and a bottle of whiskey, Edward lay in wait for the two people who could ruin his life.

Caleb and Emma opened the door to their home. Caleb was frantic to speak with Edward. He wanted to know what happened and why he didn't supervise the mine production. As Caleb rounded the bend to enter the living room, he felt the blast of the shotgun to his chest. He collapsed on the floor in a pool of blood. Emma ran to the living room and was also shot. Edward had to think, what should he do with the bodies? He didn't want anyone to know that his parents were dead. He wanted people to think they ran off to escape the lawsuits from the mine accident. Edward dragged the bodies down to the basement. He went back upstairs and scrubbed the walls and the floors of all the blood. He took their luggage into the woods. He got a shovel from the barn and buried his parents in the basement. He's very careful to pack the dirt down and hide any evidence of a fresh burial.

Leaving no valuables or evidence behind, Edward left Mingo Pond forever, never looking back and never showing any sign of remorse at taking his parents' lives. No one ever found Caleb and Emma. People assumed the house was abandoned and that Caleb and Emma left to escape lawsuits from the accident. Edward was also missing and presumed to be in hiding as well. As for the house, it lay empty. No one wanted a house that was tied to the accident at the mine and the loss of all those lives. The mine held the bodies of the miners that lost their lives in the accident. It's boarded up and abandoned. No one knew that the house at Mingo Pond also held bodies, murdered bodies.

ABOUT THE AUTHOR

LINDA HOFFMAN WAS BORN IN Homestead, Pennsylvania. She is a graduate of Bishop Boyle High School in Homestead, PA. For thirty years she has been a floral designer. For seventeen years she was the florist to the Grand Concourse in Station Square, Pittsburgh, PA. She has traveled to India to perfect her skills in Indian floral design. She is currently a floral designer at Breitinger's Flowers in White Oak, PA.

She is now in the process of developing a series of children's books. She is also the author of *He Can't Remember, She Can't Forget*.

CPSIA information can be obtained
at www.ICGtesting.com
Printed in the USA
BVHW03s0527121018
529850BV00001B/2/P

9 781681 398761